THE LEGACY DEVICE

(A DAN TAYLOR SHORT STORY)

RACHEL AMPHLETT

Copyright © 2017 by Rachel Amphlett

All rights reserved.
No part of this book may be reproduced, stored in a retrieval system, or transmitted by any means, electronic, mechanical, photocopying or otherwise, without the prior written permission of the author.

This is a work of fiction. While the locations in this book are a mixture of real and imagined, the characters are totally fictitious. Any resemblance to actual people living or dead is entirely coincidental.

FOREWORD

The Dan Taylor spy series is enthralling murder mystery readers with its fast-paced and entertaining storylines that provide a modern twist to the espionage genre.

The full-length novels are available through all major retailers and local libraries in eBook, print and audiobook.

This short story is a prequel to the first book in the series, *White Gold*.

For more information about this series and more, visit www.rachelamphlett.com.

THE LEGACY DEVICE

ONE

IRAQ, 2009

DAN TAYLOR SWORE and ducked behind the low pock-marked wall as another hail of bullets scorched across the rough terrain towards him.

'Things can't even go wrong properly around here,' he muttered.

To his left, Mitch Frazer cursed and then let loose with a quick burst from his rifle, before curling up in the culvert that ran the length of the wall, dust covering the skin around his eyes. His mouth and nose were covered by a beige-and-green-coloured scarf identical to Dan's own, a recent addition they'd adopted to counteract the choking dust from the wind-whipped sand of their environment.

Dan wondered if he looked as pissed off as Mitch did, the man's eyes blazing at him from under his scuffed standard-issue helmet.

He turned his head at a movement to his right to see their captain, David Ludlow, crawling on his elbows and knees along the line of the wall towards them.

'Status?'

'Two hostiles, stone hut to the left,' said Dan. 'Suspect three more on the perimeter at eleven o'clock.'

'Bastards.'

For a fleeting moment, Dan wondered if his superior officer referred to the idiots at Intel, who'd insisted the power facility presented no danger to the team, having been abandoned for the past two months while the local area had once more descended into chaos. Then he realised David meant the hostiles; it was simply his upbringing that prevented him from using stronger language.

Dan suppressed a smirk and instead focused on the problem at hand.

For a start, they couldn't get anywhere near the facility by firepower alone; their armoured vehicle was parked behind a building to their six o'clock position, guarded by the remaining three members of the six-man team in case one of the locals or, worse, one of their kids tried to steal it.

Their attackers had been well prepared. They'd simply waited until the three men were too far away from the safety of the vehicle to turn back, and then opened fire.

Dan, Mitch, and David had hit the ground at the first sound of trouble, only saved from instant annihilation by a combination of cover fire from the team taking cover at the vehicle's flank and the poor aim of their attackers.

'All enthusiasm, no finesse,' Mitch had grumbled as they'd crawled towards the wall they now sheltered behind.

Except their attackers were improving and showed no sign of running out of ammunition any time soon.

Unlike the team.

Even if they could somehow avoid getting shot and make their way back to the vehicle, extra ammunition was in short supply, and support from coalition troops was highly unlikely given the radio chatter they'd heard on the way over.

Something about a suicide bomber in a busy marketplace on the other side of the city.

Dan ducked as a burst of machine-gun fire exploded across the top of the wall.

'What the hell happened to "hearts and minds"?'

'This lot must've missed the lecture that day,' said Mitch.

Dan glanced at the captain who crouched at his right shoulder.

David's jaw was clenched while he rummaged in his webbing before he extracted a creased hand-drawn map. He pulled out a pen and added their current position to it, and that of the store hut. Next, Dan watched as he drew a box depicting their vehicle and then stared at the drawing from all angles before he spoke.

'All right,' he said and toggled the comms mike that hung next to his mouth. 'You getting this, Terry?'

'Copy.'

'Right,' said David. 'We'll take on the two idiots behind the stone hut. They seem better trained than the others. We'll use short bursts alternating between the three of us to keep a steady line of fire.' He cocked an eyebrow at Dan and Mitch.

Dan nodded, realising where David's tactics were leading.

'Terry, the three of you do the same to the hostiles on the perimeter. You're evenly matched, so concentrate on wearing them down.' He paused and then added. 'I have a feeling this attack is based on bravado rather than any tactical training, so let's see if we can disperse them quickly.'

David waited until each team member confirmed his understanding of the plan, then pushed his comms mike out of the way, shoved the map back into his webbing, and positioned himself against the wall, ready to strike.

'On my count, Mitch – you're up first.'

'Sir.'

'Three. Two. *One.*'

Mitch twisted his body, kept his head low, and let loose a volley of rounds at the stone hut, sending the two militants diving for cover as the dirt around them lifted into the air. He dropped behind the wall again, and Dan took his place.

As he straightened, the larger of the two men next to the hut appeared, his own weapon raised, and fired.

Dan shrank back, then gritted his teeth and took aim.

His finger placed a small amount of

pressure on the trigger, and the rifle churned in his hands.

The man stumbled back with a cry, dropping his gun and clutching the side of his face.

'Christ, did you get him?' asked Mitch.

'Shrapnel from the stonework, I think,' replied Dan.

'That'll give them something to think about,' said David, swinging his rifle in the same direction and firing.

A second cry from the injured man reached their position at the stone wall, and Dan peered over to see the man clutching his leg.

Dan's ears were already ringing from gunfire, but he could still make out the sound of rifles being fired from the direction of the vehicle. A movement to his left caught his eye, and he turned in time to see the three younger militants running away from the perimeter, cutting through the scrub and abandoned buildings in their haste to escape.

'Hold your fire,' said David, and he repeated the command through his comms mike.

Silence returned to the site, and Dan swallowed.

He could never get used to the quiet after a gunfight. Even the birds had disappeared, the blue sky above him empty, tainted by a pale hue from the dry heat that rose from the earth.

David jerked his chin towards the stone hut, where the injured man was being helped to his feet by the younger man with him.

The man raised his fist and yelled at the small group of soldiers, then ducked under the injured man's arm and helped him limp away.

'They'll be back,' said Mitch.

'Probably. No sense in hanging about to wait for them,' said David and pointed at the building. 'Let's go.'

'Just another day in paradise,' murmured Mitch as he passed Dan in a running crouch.

Dan shook his head and then followed, wondering what else was in store for them.

TWO

THE ORIGINAL ORDER TO go to the power facility had come in three hours ago, while they were preparing to leave the safety of the concrete and sand-bagged compound that was their base for the duration of their tour of duty.

Dan had been in the mess tent, tucking an extra energy bar into one of the pockets on the front of his webbing when David had approached, excitement in his eyes.

'There'll be a slight detour,' he'd said. 'Should be able to fit it in between jobs today.'

Dan had shaken his head as the young captain had grabbed an apple and then hurried out the tent towards their waiting vehicle.

'You know what that means, of course.'

THE LEGACY DEVICE

Mitch's languid tones carried across the cool space.

'Yeah. Long day,' said Dan and grabbed a second energy bar before throwing it towards the other man. 'So fuel up.'

They'd followed David across the dusty earth between the mess hut and the row of parked armoured vehicles.

When Dan had arrived at the camp on his first tour, he'd been awestruck by the sheer size of the base.

The city's airport had been used as a strategic staging post for the past six years, and since then, coalition forces had quickly sprawled over the area. Now, both the US and UK forces were withdrawing, slowly handing over more and more responsibility to the Iraqi Army.

Dan and Mitch drew level with their captain as he spoke with a major near the vehicle that had been assigned to them for the day.

The two superior officers had turned their backs after acknowledging Dan and Mitch, and as they passed, Dan strained his ears to catch what was being said.

'... try to beat the Yanks there, for Christ's

sake,' said the major. 'We'll never hear the end of it otherwise.'

'Understood,' said David. 'Is it heavily guarded?'

'Hey.' Mitch had hit Dan on the arm. 'Stop eavesdropping. It's rude.'

'Bollocks,' said Dan, but picked up his pace. If he didn't, David would know his conversation had been overheard.

'Secret stuff?'

'Yeah,' said Dan and peeled the wrapper from the top half of one of his energy bars. 'Definitely off the books, by the sound of it.'

'I'm not surprised,' said Mitch. 'I think Ludlow's got too much political ambition to stay in the army longer than he needs to.'

'Politics?' Dan checked over his shoulder. David had moved on and was deep in conversation with H, one of the other Explosive Ordnance Device operators who made up the team. 'I don't think so. PMC maybe, though?'

It was a well-known fact around the base that both UK and US private military contractors were successfully recruiting some of the best talent from the coalition forces. It wasn't a difficult career decision for some – the money was rumoured to be double, or even triple, what the armed forces paid, with better equipment and, often, better support networks.

'Not him,' said Mitch. 'Too loyal to Queen and country. Maybe the spooks will have him, though.'

'That'd make more sense.' Dan chewed through the energy bar and thought about what Mitch had said. David was certainly good at handing out information in a piecemeal fashion, keeping knowledge to himself until such time as he felt it necessary to bring his team up to speed.

Dan had simply accepted this as the man's way of working – if he thought the team needed to know something, he told them. If he didn't, well, they simply had to get on with the task at hand, trusting that he'd tell them when necessary.

Dan knew, though, that David's way of revealing information in dribs and drabs frustrated some of the team.

Especially Terry.

The older man resented the young captain's ability to read any situation quickly and effectively, even more so now that the rumours of Terry's supplying of drugs amongst some of the battalion's less savoury members had begun to circulate and pick up pace.

Dan had never managed to work out what the source of Terry's antipathy had been. He often seemed pre-occupied and sullen, reluctant to participate in the high jinks that often helped alleviate the boredom of being holed up in the heavily-fortified base in between the sheer terror of violent skirmishes and the thought of being killed.

He was certainly clever. H, the young lance corporal who had joined the small team on this current tour, was fascinated by the man's ability to reconstruct some of the IEDs they'd disarmed. When Dan had quietly voiced his concern about Terry's almost unhealthy interest in rebuilding something they'd been tasked with destroying, H had simply shrugged his shoulders.

'It helps intelligence gathering,' he'd said. 'At least this way, we get an idea of where they might be sourcing parts from – we can go after the suppliers then, rather than risking our lives dismantling the finished goods.'

Dan had let the matter rest. He had a lot of respect for the lance corporal, and unknown to H, Dan and Mitch had vowed to look out for him – with a wife and young baby back in

England, they were doing all they could to ensure he made it back to them alive, even if it meant putting their own lives in danger.

A slap on his shoulder roused him from his thoughts.

'Ready to roll?' a voice roared in his ear.

Dan grinned.

Richard 'Dicko' Henderson had been a courier driver in London prior to joining the Royal Engineers. Dan had quickly deduced that most of his stories about what he had delivered around the capital were utter bullshit, but the man was a born joker and could often be counted upon to diffuse any tension within the small team.

Dan finished the energy bar and tucked the empty wrapper into his pocket, then rubbed his eyes and tried to concentrate. Two more weeks and he'd be on leave for a month.

It wouldn't be his problem for much longer.

'Well? What do you think?' Mitch had said as they climbed into the vehicle. 'More strife for us today?'

'Definitely,' Dan had replied.

In hindsight, he realised what an understatement he'd made.

THREE

DAN LEFT the sanctuary of the stone wall and began to step carefully over the open expanse between their previous cover position and the low-set building in front of them.

His eyes swept the ground as he walked, his knuckles white as he gripped his rifle. Adrenalin coursed through his body, his chest compressing against the Kevlar jacket he wore with every deep breath.

Although the intel David had received reported no indication of any mines or other activity in the area, he wasn't prepared to take any chances.

Especially after the same intel on which they relied had failed to spot the rag-tag group of gunmen that had appeared upon their arrival.

The ground beneath his feet was uneven; a mixture of sand, stones, and dried grass that poked up from the earth, thin spindly leaves that were sharp to the touch, almost cactus-like in its ability to grow in the harshest of conditions.

Here and there, pieces of metal and twisted wire littered the dirt, slowing their progress further as they stopped to make sure no explosive ordnance was hidden amongst the debris.

Dan shifted the weight of the rifle in his hands, a headache beginning to needle the skin between his eyes. He tried to ignore it. He'd grabbed some water from his canteen, but not before they were safely within the confines of the building.

He stopped for a moment, raising his eyes to the edifice in front of them, a solid concrete monstrosity that had clearly been constructed to withstand a direct hit.

No doubt Saddam's engineers had been directed to ensure that the building would survive even the most ferocious attacks, evidenced by the fact that the structure was the only unscathed building in the immediate vicinity.

The rest of the buildings around it had

been reduced to rubble, first by the Americans' bombing campaigns and then by home-grown looters, desperate to find something to sell or barter in exchange for food and water in the days leading up to the ground troop invasion so many years ago.

Despite the silence, peppered only with the sound of his, David's, and Mitch's footsteps, there was an oppressiveness about the place, an expectancy that something was going to happen.

Dan could sense it, in the way his heartbeat rattled in his ears, the way his gut twisted.

This was different than the aftermath of a gun battle; this was the adrenalin spike of a primitive fight or flight instinct.

Every nerve in his body was telling him to run.

Instead, he twisted his neck, trying to peer past the fence and perimeter wall, but could see nothing.

'Focus.'

Mitch's voice, barely above a whisper, reached him from behind.

'I've got a bad feeling about this,' Dan murmured.

'Me, too,' said Mitch. 'So, let's get a move

on and get inside that building. We're too damn exposed out here.'

Dan exhaled and turned his attention back to the low-set building. 'What is this place, anyway?'

'A routing station,' explained David, joining them. He turned on his heel, his eyes raking the perimeter as he ran his finger under his chin-strap and loosened the material from his sweat-drenched skin and the beginnings of a beard. 'Computers,' he added. 'For their utility companies.'

'What, like water and power?' asked Dan.

'Exactly.' David checked his watch. 'Come on. Clock's ticking.'

He led the way across the forecourt of the abandoned structure and flattened his back against the chain-link fence while Mitch used wire cutters to snip a small opening for them to crawl through.

Dan went first, the sharp ends of the severed wire tearing at his jacket and webbing. Once through, he turned and kept his rifle sight trained on the scrubby trees that bordered the perimeter, watching for movement, his finger resting on the trigger guard while Mitch and David crawled through.

Mitch let the fencing fall back into place before setting off once more, and they made slow progress towards the doors of the facility in single file, a few paces away from each other.

Just in case.

Dan suppressed a yawn, the sudden fatigue taking him by surprise. He blinked rapidly and shook his head to try to clear the fogginess that was threatening to dull his senses.

Exhaustion had consumed the team for the past three weeks, sapping energy and causing friction amongst them. Arguments had broken out over the slightest of infringements, even though they all knew it was a natural reaction to the stresses of the posting.

He concentrated on the surrounding vegetation while following Mitch's footsteps, placing his boots in the tread marks left behind in the baked dirt, and vowed to devour his second energy bar the first opportunity he had.

They reached the doors without incident. Dan reached into a pouch and pulled out a length of det cord, but David held up his hand to stop him and then pointed to Mitch. 'Pick the lock. Try not to damage it.'

Dan frowned, a question forming on his tongue.

David pre-empted it. 'Orders are to try and leave no trace of us being here,' he said. 'So that means no explosives.'

Another question crossed Dan's mind, but he recalled Mitch's assertion that David would be joining the secret service at some point, so instead, he took a deep breath and concentrated on covering Mitch's back while he knelt at the door with his lock picks.

The lock gave way in under thirty seconds.

David checked his watch and then activated the comms mike tucked into his collar. 'Terry? We'll need twenty minutes. Make sure no-one else enters, or Taylor and Frazer will shoot first and ask questions later.'

'Copy that.'

Dan followed his two colleagues into the building and let the front door swing shut behind him.

Their feet echoed off the walls of the passageway as David led the way through the right-hand side of the facility.

Pockets of light entered the passageway from open doors that led to hastily abandoned offices, and Dan shook his head at the stacks of documents that had been left lying around, too late to be put through the shredding machines that had been set next to each office door.

The irony that they were in the control building for one of the provinces' biggest electricity providers, feeling their way in the gloom due to an eight-week long power cut, wasn't lost on Dan.

'What are we doing here, boss?'

David kept a brisk pace as they methodically cleared each room while progressing up the length of the corridor, farther into the heart of the building.

'This is the headquarters for one of the big electricity suppliers,' he said. 'We have to activate some of the computers.'

'How? The place is dead.'

'There should be an emergency power generator somewhere in the building,' explained David. 'But first, we need to find the main control room.'

Their boots clattered over the tiled floor as they picked up their pace, conscious of the twenty-minute deadline David had set slowly slipping away.

Finally, they turned a corner, and the passageway opened out into a large room, full of computers.

'Bingo,' said Mitch.

'Right,' said David and slung his rifle over his shoulder. 'We need to get a few of them up and running as soon as Taylor finds the auxiliary power.' He signalled to Dan. 'There should be a door leading down to a basement a little farther along the corridor. Take Mitch with you to pick the lock if necessary. Hopefully, there's a generator for emergencies that still has some diesel left in it.'

Dan nodded, spun on his heel, and led the way out of the room, hoping to hell they were long gone before the militants returned.

FOUR

THEY FOUND THE DOOR, a solid steel structure, within seconds of leaving the computer room.

Two locks sealed its contents from prying eyes, and Mitch dropped to his knees, pulling out his lock picks.

Dan watched as Mitch twisted and turned the pieces of metal within the lock, concentration etched across his features.

'Where'd you learn to do that, anyway?'

The corner of Mitch's mouth quirked. 'Let's just say I had an interesting childhood,' he said.

Dan raised an eyebrow, waiting for more, but the other man ignored him.

He waited until Mitch had picked the last of the locks on the door, then motioned to him to move aside, pulled the door open, and stared at the concrete steps leading down into darkness.

He swallowed and tried to alleviate the chill that crawled across the back of his neck.

'I'll take it from here. Go watch David's back.'

'Copy that.'

The sound of Mitch's footsteps jogging away echoed off the bare walls of the corridor, and then Dan was alone.

He checked the flashlight attached to the side of his rifle, making sure the bulb wasn't about to fade. He tweaked the weapon's position in his grip until the beam followed his line of vision, and then began the descent, his heartbeat hammering.

There was an almost prehistoric fear about going underground; Dan had never been comfortable with the whole concept – school trips to cave systems in the south of England had left him wrung out, craving daylight. Even in his previous career as a geologist, he'd had to psych himself up to descend mine shafts.

Despite the door at the top of the steps being left wide open, his imagination wreaked havoc on common sense, and he fought down the sense of panic that threatened to consume him, his breathing hard.

Sweat trickled from under his helmet and ran down one side of his face. He stopped, wiped it away, and gave himself a mental shake.

He refocused on the task at hand and turned his head to take in his surroundings.

The walls and roof of the basement were all concrete, and he suspected that the lower level had been built to withstand a direct hit from a missile. A mustiness filled the air, and he wondered how long it had been since fresh ventilation had been pumped through the shafts that peppered the ceiling.

The edge of his flashlight caught movement to his right as he reached the bottom step, and he swung round, dropping to a defensive position, rifle raised.

A fleshy tail retreated from the reach of his flashlight beam at the same time an indignant squeak reached his ears, and he mumbled a curse as the large rat scuttled off into the darkness before he straightened and took his bearings.

To his right, the beam from his flashlight reflected off the dirty metal outer casing of a diesel generator, and he hurried over to it.

He ran his hands over the back to check the exhaust hoses were attached, not wishing to asphyxiate himself as soon as he started it up, then traced their path up the wall until they disappeared through the ducting above his head.

He crossed his fingers and hit the power button, hoping David's assumption about the generator still having some diesel left in it proved correct.

He stepped back as the machine shuddered and then sprung to life, the noise filling the underground space.

Dan waited a few seconds to make sure the generator didn't suddenly stop and then turned his attention to the next task.

The basement layout was a simple box-like affair, with three enormous computer servers filling the far wall only metres from Dan's position. He strode over to them, hoping that his meagre knowledge of Arabic would suffice to work out how to power up the connection to the computer room above.

He grunted an exclamation of surprise as he neared, and the light shone off a familiar Western-based logo, the labels above switches all in English.

He ran his fingers over the dials as he read

from left to right, seeking a clue to which switch might be the main trip to the computer system, muttering under his breath.

Something ran over his foot, and he cried out and then cursed.

'Fucking rats,' he hissed.

He jumped at another squeak next to his leg, and he lashed out with his boot, connecting with something soft that scurried away, bickering between its teeth as it retreated.

He wiped sweat from his eyes and refocused on the switches.

'Come on, come on, where are you?'

He stabbed at the label when he found it, relief surging through his veins. A single switch below pointed to the "off" position, and Dan flicked it to "on".

He swung round at the sound of footsteps near the top of the steps, and then Mitch's voice carried into the darkness.

'That's it! Get back up here.'

'Copy that,' said Dan and hurried towards the relative light of the upper level.

FIVE

BY THE TIME Dan had reached the control room, David and Mitch had already bypassed the rudimentary password security of the computers' previous owners.

David had pulled a chair over to his adopted desk and was busy typing a string of code into one of the computers, the black background of the screen awash with letters and numbers that meant nothing to Dan.

'I didn't know you knew computers so well, sir,' said Mitch.

David's hands rested on the keyboard, and then he spun the chair round to face Dan and Mitch.

'What I tell you now doesn't leave this room,' he said. 'You've both signed the Official Secrets Act. Word gets out about this, it's twenty years in prison – minimum. Understand?'

Mitch nodded, while Dan's mind raced.

What the hell had David got them into?

He pushed the thought aside, relief flooding his chest that he'd insisted on taking H's place in the lead-up to the infiltration of the building. Whatever was going on here, it certainly wouldn't do the young officer's career any good.

'Understood,' he said.

'There should be enough auxiliary power from the back-up generator for what we need,' said David, reaching into his pocket.

'I'm surprised half of this stuff hasn't been taken,' Mitch murmured. 'Everything else has been torn to shit around here and sold off.'

'It still might,' said David. 'But if it isn't, then this software will kick in the moment the system's online again.'

Dan frowned. 'What's that?'

David held up a USB stick. 'Our mission,' he said and plugged the thumb drive into the nearest computer terminal.

'What do you mean?' Dan stepped closer and peered over the other man's shoulder as he punched a string of commands into the keyboard.

'This, and Afghanistan will probably be one of the last conflicts whole countries will get involved with,' he said. He pointed at the computer screen as it flickered to life. 'This is the future, Taylor. Countries infiltrating each other's networks. Cyber warfare.'

David's fingers pecked at the keyboard as he spoke. 'Certain people believe it's a good idea to keep an eye on Iraqi installations such as this once we're out of the country,' he said. 'They believe that by spying on the utility companies, they'll be able to head off any repeat of someone like Saddam Hussain exerting too much influence in the region.'

Dan folded his arms across his chest and frowned. 'How?'

David stopped typing. 'There's a program on here, a specialised one, that'll track keystrokes on these computers once we load it into the system. We only need to apply it to the ones here – the program will seek out the others in the building through the servers once the main power is switched back on. Whenever that happens.'

He typed a command and sat back in his chair. 'Takes fifteen minutes to download and distribute,' he explained.

'Wait, so you're saying whoever wrote that

program will be able to control this facility?' asked Mitch.

'Yes. And if anyone like Saddam Hussain gets into power again, they'll be able to shut it down, too,' said David.

'Why today?' asked Dan.

'Three reasons,' said David. 'First of all, the software had to be designed and then encrypted so it can't be located in the system once this place goes live. It only arrived last night. Second, it'll help British interests get a toe-hold in the rebuilding of the country. No-one else will be able to work around this coding – it'll throw up too many issues. Third, there's going to be a public announcement from the Prime Minister tomorrow that more British troops are going to be pulled out of Basra.' His eyes held Dan's. 'And there's no way in hell the British secret service was going to let the Americans get to this stuff first.'

Dan rocked back on his heels, his heart thumping.

They'd all heard the reports about the number of British and American companies baying at the thought of lucrative contracts for the rebuilding of Iraq.

Dan frowned. 'So, we're not the only ones doing this?'

'Correct. Every British patrol that's out today will be visiting a pre-defined facility,' replied David. He paused. 'Every facility we've got control of, anyway,' he added.

'You call this control?' hissed Mitch. 'We nearly got killed getting in here.'

Dan reached out and punched him on the arm. 'Steady,' he said.

'If we don't do this, they will,' said David. 'It's a mess. It's going to go on for years, and I don't think we'll ever fully appreciate the impact we've had on the region until it's too late.'

Dan turned back, surprised at his senior officer's frankness, and then realised that Mitch was probably right.

David was up to his neck in it. Spies and all.

Dan bit off a retort as Mitch's radio crackled to life and the man stepped away, murmuring into his comms mike. The man's eyes opened wide, and for the first time in his life, Dan saw Mitch's face pale beyond recognition.

He ran to the window, his rifle raised, and then glanced over his shoulder to where

David sat, before turning his attention back to the perimeter of the property. His eyebrows shot up.

'Er, boss. We've got company.'

'I need another ten minutes.'

'I don't think you're going to get them.' Mitch swore and spun away from the glass window as it disintegrated, sending shards across his boots. His eyes were wide. 'They've brought all their friends with them.'

'It wasn't a request.'

'Dammit, I thought not,' Mitch hissed.

Dan ran to the window opposite and edged around the sill. 'I've got one tango approaching my side.'

'Armed?'

'Can't see a weapon. Hang on.' Dan squinted against the bright light as the man's hand moved to his side. 'Ah, shit.'

'What is it?' David's voice echoed off the walls.

'Petrol bomb.'

'Shit.' David tapped his comms mike. 'Terry? What the hell is going on out there?'

The man's response filled all their earpieces.

'We're coming under fire from several

hostiles,' he said. 'Multiple locations. Recommend immediate evacuation.'

A bead of sweat ran down Dan's cheek, and he wiped it away, his headache returning in earnest.

SIX

'Okay,' said David. 'Change of plan.' He pulled an identical USB stick from the front flap of his jacket. 'We'll have to do this manually rather than waiting for one computer to do all the work for us.'

Dan took the item that David held out to him. 'What do I do?'

'Plug it into each computer in turn. Hit the 'escape' button. Wait until the screen goes blank. Then take the stick out and move to the next machine.'

'Do I switch the machine off afterwards?'

'No need. We'll just turn off the auxiliary power once we're finished.'

'Got it.'

'Good. Then hurry,' said David.

'Otherwise, we're going to have a problem bigger than *Ben Hur*.'

Mitch's voice carried across to Dan as he worked. 'What did people say before that film came out?'

'What?'

'*Ben Hur*. The movie. What did people say before the movie came out? If something was bigger than *Ben Hur*?'

Dan stared at him. 'Are you serious?'

Mitch shrugged. 'These things make me think.'

'Mitch?'

'Yeah?'

'Stop thinking.'

'Enough, you two,' snapped David. 'We're running out of time.' He tapped the outer casing of the USB stick in the computer next to him, a green LED flashing on its end. 'Come *on*,' he urged.

Dan rubbed his earlobe between his finger and thumb.

David noticed his reticence and shrugged. 'It's us or them,' he said. 'There are too many countries in this coalition, and God knows how many hangers-on. When this country ramps up again, we *have* to make sure we can protect its interests.'

And ours, Dan thought.

He shook his head. 'So where does that leave us?'

'Alive,' Mitch called over from the other side of the room. 'Behind a desk.' He swore as a series of bullets peppered the window frame next to him and then fired his weapon through the opening. 'And not dealing with this shit on a daily basis. *Fuck*. They're getting closer!'

Dan clenched his teeth and ran to the next desk, inserting the USB stick. He waited until the screen went blank, as David said it would, and then moved to the next.

Moments later, he had reached the far end of the control room.

'How many more, Taylor?' called David.

'Six on this side.'

'Go and help Frazer. I'll do those.'

Dan checked the magazine in his rifle, replaced it with a fresh clip, and hurried to where Mitch stood firing short bursts of rounds through the now-unglazed window.

His feet scuffed over debris, broken chairs, and loose stationery that had been discarded by the employees of the facility in their rush to flee. Here and there, remnants of glass clinked under his step.

A hot breeze filtered through the space as he approached, and he stepped out of the direct line of the window, in case one of the hostiles got a lucky shot.

Instead, he hung to the right of the room and took up position with his shoulder brushing the bare wall.

As Dan settled his weight and raised his rifle, Mitch quickly appraised him of the situation.

'Four hostiles on this side of the building. Terry and the others have the rest covered – about twelve trying to reach the perimeter.'

Dan fought down the panic that rose in his chest. If the hostiles managed to breach the perimeter and reach the front door, the three of them would be sitting ducks.

He swung out from behind the window frame and aimed at the militant between the sights of his scope. He lowered his aim a little and then fired.

The man slumped to the floor, clutching his leg. Not dead, but not going to get up and continue fighting either if the shouting from outside was any indication.

The hostile next to him stopped firing at the building, dragged his colleague out of range, and then returned and began shooting once more at their position.

'Will you stop hitting them in the legs?' said Mitch. 'It just pisses them off!'

Dan smirked. In a sense, the man was right, but he couldn't bring himself to kill. Not yet.

Their radios crackled once more.

'We're coming under heavy fire out here,' H reported and then swore loudly. 'You need to hurry.'

'We're done,' confirmed David and pulled the two USB sticks from the computers, placing them back in his pocket. 'Taylor, go and switch off the power,' he said. 'And don't hang about.'

'On it.'

Dan ran through the room, down the corridor, and slid to a halt next to the open door to the basement, stalling his momentum by reaching out and grabbing a hold of the door frame.

He flicked on his flashlight and hurried down the steps, ignoring the scraping and scuttling noises from the concrete floor beneath his boots as the rats ran for cover.

He slammed the palm of his hand against the front of the controls for the servers and pushed the button to power down the system once more.

Next, he turned off the generator.

It cut out with an audible groan, and Dan stepped back, the light on his rifle illuminating the dials and switches a final time while he satisfied himself the system wouldn't switch itself on once they'd exited the building.

He nodded, spun on his heel, and took the stairs two at a time, breathing a sigh of relief when he reached the top step. He pushed the door closed behind him, tugged at the door handle to make sure it held firm, and then ran back to the control room, the sound of gunfire reverberating in the enclosed space.

SEVEN

'Sir? Sir?'

Terry's voice carried through their earpieces.

'What?'

'I think I can create a distraction – give you some time to get out of there.'

'How?' David's forehead creased, and he raised an eyebrow when he saw Dan looking in his direction.

'We've got det cord here. A few stones and rocks,' said Terry. 'Leave it with me, and I'll make sure this mob stay clear for a little while.'

David covered his comms mike with his hand and paced the space in front of the computer.

Mitch frowned. 'You okay with this, boss?'

David rubbed his hand over his face. 'Do you have a better idea?'

Both Dan and Mitch fell silent.

'Thought not.' David pressed his comms mike. 'You can do it safely? Without causing injuries to the team?'

'Yes, sir.' Terry's voice echoed across the airwaves within the abandoned room. 'It'll take me thirty seconds to set it up.'

'Okay. Do it.'

'Sir.'

Dan crouched and made his way back to the window.

He'd often wondered if Terry's preoccupation with explosives was healthy.

After all, it was one thing to learn as much as possible about what was being used to create the various different kinds of IEDs. It was quite another to take those parts and successfully recreate the bombs the team worked so hard to destroy.

He'd asked one day, trying to fathom the older man's obsession.

Terry had shrugged. 'There's fuck all else to do around here,' he'd growled.

Now, Dan figured it'd be a bonus if Terry's tinkering around with leftover bomb parts meant a chance for them to escape the power facility intact.

The fire flared next to the window frame, and Dan fell back as Mitch cursed, the stench of petrol filling the air.

'You okay?' Dan yelled, staggering to his feet.

'No,' shouted Mitch. 'I'm pissed off.'

Dan aimed his weapon through the opening and let loose two quick rounds.

A muffled cry carried on the wind, and he threw himself back against the wall.

'Hurry up, Terry,' he murmured.

In response, a loud *crack* from the other side of the building reached his ears, swiftly followed by another.

'What the hell was that?'

Dan shook his head. 'I don't know.'

Heavy gunfire followed the third *crack*, and it dawned on him.

'Terry.'

'What's he doing?'

'Hang on.'

Dan left Mitch covering the window and hurried through the control room and past David, who didn't even glance up from his position at the far window, his face a mask of concentration as he stared down the sight of his rifle and fired.

He reached the far wall and edged to the window, in time to see a glimpse of British Army combat fatigues identical to his own flash past the perimeter behind an angry mob of hostiles, all aiming their rag-tag collection of weapons at the building.

Some carried bottles with dirty cloths protruding from the necks, held perilously close to waving cigarette lighters.

And then all hell broke loose – the dirt behind the crowd seemed to lift upwards at their feet, followed by a familiar *crack*, and a fountain of stones and loose gravel shot between their legs.

Those lucky enough to be far enough away ran to one side before taking up their angry chants once more, only for a second *crack* to fill the air.

'What's he doing?' asked David.

'I *think* he's tied plastique around some rocks with det cord,' said Dan. He shook his head in wonder. 'It seems to be working.'

Slowly, the mob fell apart, the less rowdy members losing momentum as their leaders limped away, clutching pock-marked legs and arms.

Dan exhaled, watched the last of the

hostiles disperse, and then turned back to the room.

David jerked his head towards the door.

'We're all done here. Let's go before they bring back the real reinforcements.'

EIGHT

THE SOUND of heavy breathing filled the space as the four passengers in the rear of the armoured vehicle tried to get their nerves under control. The jokes and banter would return in time, but for now, the team retreated into themselves while they processed each aspect of the gunfight.

The viciousness of the attack had rattled them all, and Dan had to admit that without Terry's quick-thinking, the outcome could have been very different.

He closed his eyes and rocked his head from side to side, rolling his shoulders to loosen tight muscles.

His thoughts returned to the power facility and what David had done.

Hell of a legacy to leave behind, he thought and then opened his eyes.

Mitch sat opposite and cocked an eyebrow.

Dan shook his head. They'd talk later, in private, about what they had seen, but not before.

Not with the threat of imprisonment hanging over their heads.

He swallowed and wondered what other nefarious activities he'd be drawn into before he returned to England in two weeks' time, and whether he'd have a choice in any of it.

He suspected not.

His body rocked to the left as Dicko swung the vehicle in a wide arc and then brought it to a standstill. He held his breath until he heard the driver shout from the front seat.

'All clear!'

H was closest to the back door, and he pushed it open, bright sunlight bathing the rear of the vehicle.

Dan held up his hand to shade his eyes as he climbed out. Despite his sunglasses, the glare from the sun glancing off the sand was intense.

The rest of the team emerged from the vehicle, and Dan pulled a canteen of water from his pack, then rummaged around inside until he found some painkillers.

Gulping the tablets, he finished half the water before coming up for air and wiped the back of his hand across his mouth.

The sound of H's voice from the front cab of the vehicle carried on the wind towards him, and he tore open the wrapper to the last of his energy bars, devouring the contents as quickly as possible.

Just because they'd had a narrow escape didn't mean they'd get an early pass back to base, and they could be out for hours yet.

He jumped at a tap on his elbow and spun round to see Terry beckoning to him as he walked a small distance from the vehicle and the group of men surrounding it.

Dan sighed and tucked the empty wrapper into his webbing. He could guess what Terry wanted to talk about.

He trudged after the older man, who stopped next to a burnt-out old car and waited for Dan to join him.

'Terry.'

'What happened?'

'What do you mean?'

'You know what I mean. In the power facility. What was Ludlow up to?'

Dan rubbed his hand over his jaw. 'I don't know,' he said. 'Mitch and I were just there to provide cover.'

'Bullshit.'

'Terry? If you're so worried about it, why don't you ask him yourself?'

He saw the other man's jaw clench, his bluff called.

Anger flashed in his eyes, and he glared past Dan towards their vehicle.

Dan decided to change the subject. 'That was one hell of a stunt you pulled back there,' he said. 'But don't you think it's a bit unhealthy messing about with the stuff we're trying to stop from exploding?'

Terry shrugged and gazed past Dan towards the dusty road bordered by abandoned houses and derelict shops. 'Someone out there is supplying them.'

'Well, hopefully, once this drugs investigation is over, you can find out who it is.'

Terry's lip curled. 'Nothing's been proven,' he said. 'And they've got nothing on me.'

Dan held up his hands. 'I didn't say they did.'

Terry ignored him, spun on his heel, and stalked back to their vehicle.

'Careful,' Mitch said, wandering over to where he'd been standing, his rifle slung between his arms as his eyes scanned the horizon.

'Trouble?'

'I've got a bad feeling about that one,' said Mitch. 'Never been able to work him out.'

'You think the rumours are true?'

'About the drugs?'

'Yeah.'

'Maybe.' Mitch slapped Dan on the back. 'Not our problem.'

They fell silent at the sound of the vehicle's radio crackling to life.

Here comes the next one, Dan thought.

David took the radio from H and spoke to the intelligence officer at the other end.

Dan's heartbeat began to rise once more, the adrenalin coursing through his system as he waited to hear where they'd be sent next.

As soon as the radio operator finished, David turned to face the five expectant faces.

'We've got a live one,' he confirmed.

'Where?' asked Dan, already reaching up to the back of the vehicle and ready to climb in.

'About six kilometres from here,' said H. 'Someone's kid has reported seeing a small group burying a roadside device. It's outside of our usual area, but there's no-one else available.'

'Right, let's go,' said David. 'Before that kid gets hurt.'

Dan hauled himself up into the vehicle, grabbed a seat near the front, and then turned to Mitch and grinned.

'Looks like we're back in business.'

THE END

ABOUT THE AUTHOR

Rachel Amphlett is a USA Today bestselling author of crime fiction and spy thrillers, many of which have been translated worldwide.

Her novels are available in eBook, print, and audiobook formats from libraries and retailers as well as her website shop.

A keen traveller, Rachel has both Australian and British citizenship.

Find out more about Rachel's books at: www.rachelamphlett.com.

www.ingramcontent.com/pod-product-compliance
Lightning Source LLC
LaVergne TN
LVHW042002060526
838200LV00041B/1828